Graphic design and illustrations: Zapp
Story adaptation: Jane Brierley

© 1996 Tormont Publications Inc.
   338 Saint Antoine St. East
   Montreal, Canada H2Y 1A3
   Tel. (514) 954-1441
   Fax (514) 954-5086

Printed in China

THE LITTLE TIN SOLDIER

TORMONT

Once upon a time, a tinsmith made a set of toy soldiers out of some old tin. The soldiers stood very straight, each carrying a gun on his shoulder, and they wore smart red jackets, blue trousers and tall black hats with gold badges on the front. There wasn't quite enough tin to finish the last soldier, however, so he had only one leg.

The tinsmith then took the soldiers to a toy shop and very soon they were bought as a birthday present for a small boy. The one-legged soldier was the first to be taken out of the box as the boy opened his presents in front of his brother and sister.

The soldier found himself facing a paper castle with glass swans floating around it on a little glass lake. But the loveliest toy of all was a little paper ballerina with a pink muslin skirt, standing at the castle door. A big sequin twinkled on her blue sash. The little dancer held her arms above her and lifted her leg behind her so that it was hidden.

"That's the girl for me!" thought the soldier, believing she was one-legged like himself.

That night, when all the people in the house had gone to bed, the toys began to play. The nutcracker did somersaults while the other toys danced and ran about. The only toys that didn't move were the tin soldier and the lovely paper ballerina. They just stood and gazed at each other.

Suddenly, the clock struck midnight and, with a *snap!*, the jack-in-the-box lid flew back and a wicked-looking goblin sprang up.

"Keep your eyes to yourself, tin soldier!" he cried. But the soldier just kept staring straight ahead.

"Very well. Just wait until tomorrow!" growled the goblin.

The next morning, the little boy played with his soldier for a while, then put him on the sill by the open window. Perhaps it was the wind, or perhaps it was the goblin, but before he knew it, the soldier was blown out of the window. The little boy ran to the window and looked out. He stared at the street, three floors below, but couldn't see anything.

"Please, couldn't I go down and look for my soldier?" he asked the maid. But she shook her head. It was raining much too hard for the little boy to go outside.

The maid shut the window firmly, leaving the little boy looking sadly through the windowpane.

Down below, two street urchins were playing in the rain. They found the tin soldier, wedged upside-down with his gun stuck between two paving stones.

"Let's make him a boat!" they cried, for the street gutter was so full that it had become a real stream. Taking an old newspaper, they folded it into a paper hat, tucked the soldier into the brim, then set the hat afloat in the gutter.

The soldier stood erect, staring straight ahead as his boat rushed along. The next thing he knew, it had drifted into a long dark drain.

"Where am I going now?" he sighed. "This must be the goblin's fault. If only the beautiful ballerina were here with me, I wouldn't mind."

Just then a huge rat rose up beside the boat. "Stop! Where's your passport?" it screeched. But the boat rushed on, going faster and faster.

The paper boat tumbled out of the drain and into the canal. By now it was so soggy that it couldn't stay afloat. Finally, it fell apart and the tin soldier, standing as straight as ever, sank down, down, down...but almost at once he was gobbled up by a big fish.

"How dark it is in here!" he thought. "Even darker than in my box!"

The fish swam down the canal and out to sea, carrying the tin soldier in its stomach. The soldier dreamed of the big room with the children, the toys, the paper castle, and the lovely ballerina.

"I guess I'll never see them again — never see *her* again," he sighed. He couldn't imagine where he was or what was happening to him. But, as luck would have it, the fish swam into a net and was soon hauled aboard a fishing boat.

The boat brought its catch back to the city and the fish was laid out in the fishmonger's stall. Before long, who should come by but the maid from the little boy's house to choose the biggest fish — the one with the soldier inside.

The maid then delivered the fish to the cook. "What a fine fish!" exclaimed the cook, as she slit open the fish's stomach to prepare it for the oven. "But there's something hard in here," she muttered. Then, to her surprise, she pulled out the tin soldier.

The maid recognized it right away. "It's the young master's lost soldier!" she cried.

The little boy was very happy when he heard that his lost soldier had been found. As for the tin soldier, he was a little dizzy at first from the bright light, after being so long in the dark. Finally, he realized where he was.

He saw the very same toys on the table, and the pretty paper castle with its glass lake. Right in front of him was the lovely dancer, still standing on one leg. If he'd had any extra tin for tears, he would have wept. Instead, he just gazed at her, and she gazed back.

All of a sudden, the little boy's brother grabbed the tin soldier.

"Ugh!" he shouted. "This soldier's no good. He's only got one leg. And besides, he smells like fish!"

And much to everyone's horror, the angry child threw the tin soldier into the fire.

Landing upright, the tin soldier glowed brightly in the flames, but his colors disappeared as he began to melt. Suddenly, a puff of wind blew the little dancer off the castle steps, and like a bird she flew into the fire with him. One bright flare...and she was gone.

In the morning, the maid emptied the grate. Among the ashes she found a lump of tin shaped like a heart, and beside it, burnt black as coal, lay the ballerina's sequin.